Based on the bestselling children's book series by Anna Dewdney

llama llama

Anna Dewdney

5-minute stories

PENGUIN YOUNG READERS LICENSES
An Imprint of Penguin Random House LLC, New York

The stories in this book were originally published individually as follows: *Llama Llama and Friends* in 2017 by Penguin Young Readers Licenses; *Llama Llama and the Lucky Pajamas*, *Llama Llama Learns to Swim*, and *Llama Llama Loves Camping* in 2018 by Penguin Young Readers Licenses; *Llama Llama Be My Valentine!* and *Llama Llama Loses a Tooth* in 2018 by Penguin Young Readers; and *Llama Llama Happy Birthday!* in 2019 by Penguin Young Readers Licenses.

Llama Llama and Friends illustrated by JJ Harrison.

This 5-Minute Stories edition published in 2019 by Penguin Young Readers Licenses, an imprint of Penguin Random House LLC, New York. Manufactured in China.

Visit us online at www.penguinrandomhouse.com.

Proprietary ISBN 9780593090084   10 9 8 7 6 5 4 3 2 1

CONTENTS

llama llama learns to swim

Anna Dewdney

Llama Llama and his friends play in Luna Giraffe's backyard. Luna shows everyone her brand-new swimsuit.

"I have an idea!" she says. "Let's go to the beach!"

"A beach day sounds like fun!" says Nelly Gnu.

"We can go bodyboarding."

Gilroy, Euclid, and Luna are excited. But

Llama Llama isn't so sure.

"You look nervous, Llama Llama," says

Nelly. "Don't you want to go to the beach?"

"Well," says Llama. "I don't know if I like the beach. But it could be fun, right?"

"It's going to be a blast!" says Nelly.

That night, Llama Llama talks to Mama Llama. He tells her he is worried about going to the beach. "I'm afraid to go in the water," he says.

Mama Llama puts her arm around Llama's shoulder.

"Is that because you don't know how to swim?" she asks.

Llama nods.

"It's okay, honey," says Mama Llama.

"Not knowing how to swim is nothing to be

ashamed of. Would you like me to give you

a swimming lesson?"

"Yes!" exclaims Llama Llama.

The next day, Llama and Mama go to

Eleanor Elephant's house. She has a pool!

Llama dips a foot in the water.

"Not bad, right?" asks Mama Llama.

"Actually, it's pretty nice!" says Llama.

Mama shows Llama some swimming strokes. Then Mama helps Llama float on the water. Finally, they both hold their breath and dip underwater together. Llama Llama likes learning to swim!

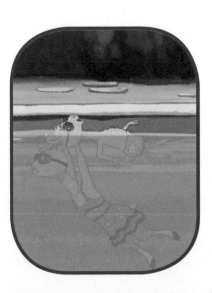

After their lesson, Llama and his Mama

say "Goodbye!" and "Thank you!" to Eleanor.

As they are leaving, Nelly and Luna walk by.

"What were you two doing at Eleanor

Elephant's house?" Luna asks.

Llama tells his friends the truth. "Mama was giving me a swimming lesson," he admits. "I was nervous about going to the beach because I don't know how to swim."

"We could all use a little practice before hitting the waves," says Nelly. "Mama Llama, will you give us a lesson, too?"

Mama Llama agrees.

The next day, Llama's friends join him

for another swimming lesson. There's even

a surprise guest—Grandpa Llama!

Llama is confused. "Grandpa, what are

you doing here?" he asks.

"Your mama told me you were afraid of getting in the water," says Grandpa. "Well, so am I! I never learned how to swim."

Llama Llama smiles. He can't believe it! But he's glad to have a swim buddy who is just as nervous as he is.

"We'll stick together, kiddo!" says Grandpa.

Llama and his friends practice different kinds of swimming strokes. Luna shows everyone how to dog-paddle. She kicks her legs and paddles her hands underwater.

Everyone else gives it a try. Dog-paddling is fun!

"Grandpa," says Llama, "we're *llama*-paddling!"

Grandpa laughs.

By the end of their lesson, Llama Llama

and Grandpa Llama swim all the way across

the pool. "You did it!" everyone cheers.

"You swim buddies are ready for the

beach tomorrow!" Nelly says.

The next day at the beach, Llama Llama's friends are by his side.

"Don't worry," says Nelly. "You can do it."

"Just remember everything you learned at the pool," says Euclid.

"Okay," says Llama. He takes a deep breath. "Here goes!"

Llama wades into the water. It is cold

and wet. The sand squishes under his feet.

It feels great!

But something is missing—his swim

buddy! "Where's Grandpa?" Llama asks.

Llama sees his grandpa standing at the

shore. He is scared to get in the water!

"Oh no!" says Llama. "I have to help him!"

"There's a lot more water here than there was in the pool," Grandpa says nervously.

Llama Llama takes his grandpa's hand.

"It's okay," says Llama. "I'm your swim buddy, remember? I'll be right by your side."

Grandpa nods. "You're right," he says. "Let's do it!"

"One foot at a time," Llama says as they

walk into the water.

"Hey, this feels pretty nice!" says Grandpa.

"Especially because we're doing it

together," says Llama.

Llama Llama and Grandpa Llama float
on the water. They toss a beach ball back
and forth with Llama's friends. They're
having so much fun! And then . . .

. . . they go bodyboarding!

"Everybody ready?" asks

Nelly. "Here comes the wave!"

Llama cheers. "Woo-hoo!"

"We're doing it!" says

Grandpa.

Later, Llama Llama and Grandpa Llama
visit Mama and Grandma Llama on the
beach. "I'm really proud of you!" says
Mama. "You faced your fears and got in
the water. And now here you are, playing
and swimming with everyone."

Llama Llama and Grandpa Llama both

feel proud. "Thanks, Mama!" says Llama.

"I guess you *can* teach an old llama new

tricks!" says Grandpa.

"There's just one problem," says Grandpa Llama. "We don't ever want to go home!"

llama llama and friends

Anna Dewdney

Llama Llama's eyes
pop open as the morning
sun warms his face.

He hops into his
overalls and rushes
downstairs. Mama Llama
needs his help today.

"Mama," Llama asks, "is your list ready?"

"Breakfast before errands," says Mama

Llama, spooning out his oatmeal. "Little

helpers need lots of energy!"

After breakfast, Llama ties a basket to

his scooter. He tucks in Fuzzy with the list.

"Let's go!"

Dion dances over. "**QUACK! QUACK!**"

"I'll be home soon," Llama tells him.

"You keep Mama company."

Llama sings as he zooms along.

It's so much fun having errands to run!

At the store, he bumps into his friend Euclid.

"Hey, Llama. I'm buying a puzzle," says Euclid. "What are you shopping for?"

Llama checks his list. "Streamers. Why would Mama need them?"

"Hmm." Euclid blinks, thinking hard. "To fancy up your front yard? Or to perk up her pink car?"

Llama and Euclid peek and poke in every

aisle. Finally, they find the streamers.

Euclid pays for his puzzle. He helps

Llama count his coins.

Outside, Euclid says, "Let's do this puzzle together!"

"Later," Llama promises, waving his list. Then he

scooters off down the hill.

It's so much fun
having errands to run!

At Daddy Gnu's Bakery, Llama's best

buddy, Nelly Gnu, flings open the door.

"Llama!" she cries. "I need your help! I'm

painting a mural."

"Okay," Llama says, taking a brush and

dipping it in the paint. Together they paint

pies, pastries, and cupcakes.

After a while, Llama stands back.

"These look yummy!" he says, gazing at

their work.

"Oh no!"

"What?" asks Nelly.

"I forgot!" cries Llama. "I'm here to buy some cupcakes."

He squeezes the box into his basket.

"See you soon," Nelly calls as Llama scooters away.

Llama struggles up What-a-View Hill,

huffing and puffing.

He flops down at the top.

Thump! Thump! Thump! What was that?

Gilroy Goat is kicking a soccer ball against a tree trunk.

"Hi, Gilroy!" Llama greets his classmate.

"It's Gilroy *the Great*!" Gilroy brags, bouncing

the ball off the tree again. "Bet you can't do this!"

Llama just has to try. The score is tied when Llama's list blows past him, carried by a strong breeze.

"My list!" he cries, scooping it up. "Sorry, Gilroy, I have to run!" Llama jumps back on the scooter.

It's so much fun
having errands to run!

Llama zooms back down the hill and slides to a stop at the farm of Gram and Grandpa Llama.

Gram shuts off the tractor. "A visit from Llama!" she exclaims happily.

Llama gives Gram a big hug, and then holds out his list. "Mama said you have the colored paper that she needs."

"Yes, here it is." Grandpa hands Llama a pile of colorful paper.

"Thanks!" says Llama. He kisses Gram and Grandpa goodbye and hurries on his way.

It's so much fun having errands to run!

As Llama passes the park, his good
friend Luna runs over from the slide.

"Llama, can you play?"

"I'm busy getting stuff for Mama," he
replies. "But I'm almost done."

"Flowers," Luna reads from the list. "I'll help you pick some!" She gathers a bunch of flowers and makes a bouquet.

While Luna picks, Llama plays on the slide, whooping and giggling.

Luna hands Llama the bouquet. He calls,

"Thanks, Luna!" and pushes off as fast as he can.

It's so much fun having errands to run!

As he rides by the school, he glances at the clock. He's been gone too long! Mama Llama will be worried!

But when he arrives home, Mama isn't waiting at the gate, or peeking out the window, or opening the door.

Llama bursts in.

"SURPRISE!"

shouts everyone.

Llama is speechless!

"It's a party for *you*, Llama," Mama says, "to thank you for always being such a good helper!"

She gives him a big hug.

THANK YOU, LLAMA!

Everyone helps set up the party supplies

that Llama brought home.

Euclid hangs streamers.

Nelly arranges cupcakes.

Luna places flowers in a vase.

And Gilroy makes hats from the colored

paper.

"**QUACK! QUACK!**" says Dion,

jiggling the balloons.

Llama laughs and puts on a party hat.

My errands are done
and we're ALL having fun!

llama llama

Anna Dewdney

llama loses a tooth

Llama Llama carries a box of his toys.

Mama Llama carries a box, a bag, and a

ball.

Crash!

"Sorry!" says Mama.

"I don't want to bump my loose tooth,"

says Llama.

He wants it to fall out on its own.

He will put it under his pillow.

Llama smiles at Mama.

"Oh no, Llama. Your tooth already fell

out!" Mama says.

But where did it go?

They remember the places they visited

that day . . .

Nelly Gnu's house, Luna Giraffe's house,

Daddy Gnu's bakery, and the park.

Mama hugs Llama. "Don't worry. We'll

look here first," she says.

Mama shakes Llama's bed blanket.

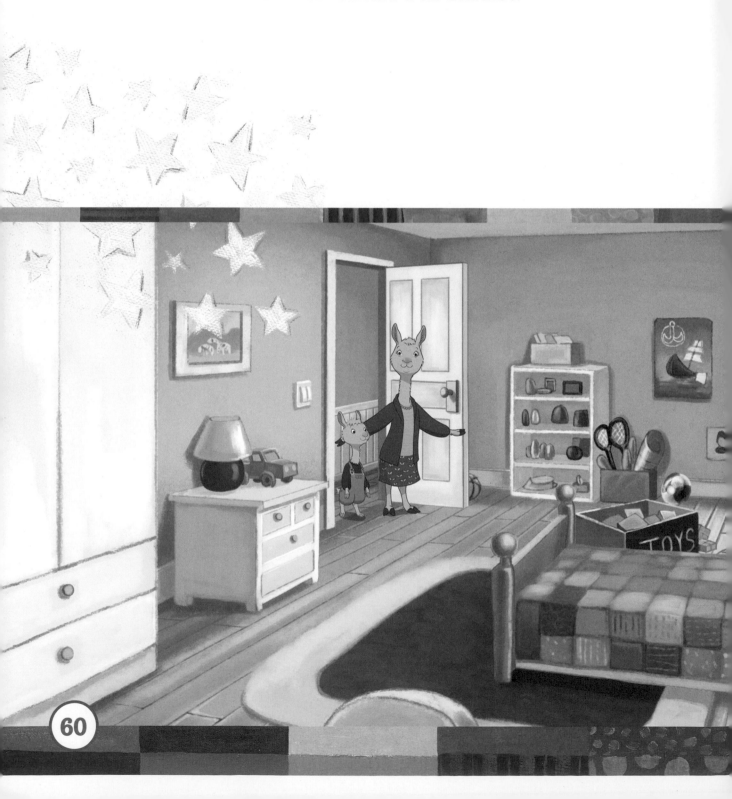

Llama plays while they look.

They have fun.

But they don't find Llama's tooth.

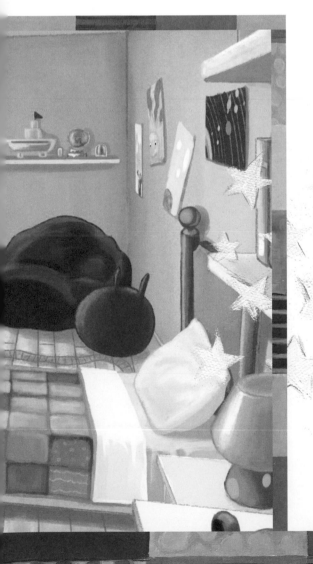

Next they look in the kitchen.

Llama sees his reflection in the kettle.

His ears droop.

"Oh, where is my tooth?" he moans.

Mama and Llama visit Nelly Gnu.

They look in her yard.

Llama finds an earthworm.

Llama finds a pretty pebble.

They swing high to look more.

Whee!

Whoopee!

They have fun.

But they don't find Llama's

tooth.

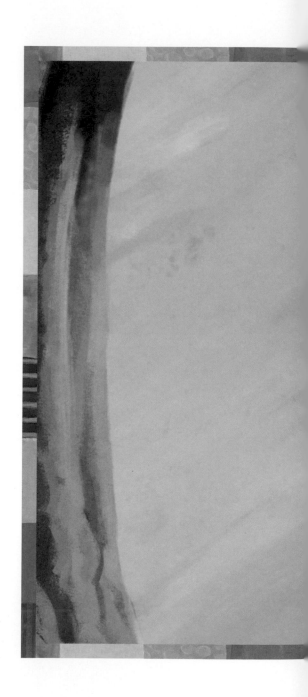

Then they visit Luna.

"I found the tooth!" cries Nelly.

"Sorry," says Luna. "Those are beads for my art."

Mama Llama hugs Llama. "We'll keep looking," she says.

They visit Daddy Gnu's bakery.

The tooth is not there.

More friends join the
hunt.

They go to the park.

They march around
and look for the tooth.

They have fun.

But they don't find
Llama's tooth.

They look in the sandbox.

Harry the Arctic Hare helps, too.

"I found it!" calls Harry. "But it is only

a piece of shell."

Harry gives Llama ice cream to cheer

him up.

Then Llama Llama remembers.

"We went to Gram and Grandpa's

house," he says.

There they check the yard and kitchen.

They don't find Llama's tooth.

Everyone goes back to Llama's house to look some more.

They find many lost things.

But they don't find Llama's tooth.

Llama is sad at bedtime.

Then he hears music outside.

Gram is playing her flute.

Gram says, "My flute made awful noises tonight. And when I turned it over, look what popped out!"

Gram hands it to Mama.

It's Llama Llama's tooth!

Then Llama remembers.

He blew on Gram's flute in her kitchen!

His tooth must have fallen out then.

Finally, Llama puts the tooth under his

pillow.

In the morning, Llama checks under his pillow.

The tooth is gone, but now there are coins instead. "Yippee!" he cheers.

llama llama
be my valentine!

Llama Llama is at school.

He is happy.

Tomorrow is Valentine's Day!

He jumps for joy.

Zelda Zebra is Llama Llama's teacher.

"Valentine's Day is a day to share how

much you care," says Zelda Zebra.

"To celebrate, we are going to have a
party!" says Zelda Zebra.

Each person in Llama's class will make a

special gift to bring to the party.

It is time to have fun and be creative!

Zelda Zebra tells everyone to make

something that only *they* can make.

Luna Giraffe is busy with her crafts.

She uses glitter, ribbon, and colored paper.

Gilroy Goat looks sadly at his friend Luna.

"I have no idea what gift to make," he says.

"I'm not very good with glitter."

Gilroy is worried. What will he make for his

friends?

Llama Llama can help.

"There are so many other things to

make," says Llama.

How about a sculpture from clay?

Oh no!

"I made a blob," says Gilroy.

"Maybe I should try something besides

art," he says.

Llama Llama goes home after school.

He wants to make his Valentine's gifts

with Mama Llama.

Llama Llama invites Gilroy to his house to help.

Maybe that will give Gilroy a new idea of something he can make.

Llama says that he has an idea.

Llama wants to make yummy cookies for
his friends.

"I can make them heart-shaped!" he says.

"I'm ready to help," says Mama Llama.

"Me too!" shouts Gilroy.

Uh-oh!

Making cookies isn't so easy.

"Our cookies look like blobs!" says Llama Llama.

Mama Llama has an idea.

"I say we make another batch," she says.

Next time they will look like hearts.

Llama Llama and Gilroy take a break

from baking to visit Luna.

She is making animals out of

paper for her gifts.

"I knew you would

make something fantastic!"

says Llama Llama.

"You are always so

creative!"

The boys try to make a paper bird.

Oh no!

Gilroy's bird doesn't look like a bird at all!

"I better keep trying to find something

else I'm good at," says Gilroy.

At home, Llama Llama and Gilroy make

another batch of cookies.

Oh no!

These cookies do not look like hearts,

either!

"This cookie looks like an octopus!" Llama says as he looks at his cookies.

"Don't worry. We will try again," says Mama.

"While these cookies are baking, let's go visit Nelly to see what she is making," says Llama.

Llama and Gilroy go to Nelly's house.

"It smells so good in here!" says Gilroy.

"We're using cookie cutters to make

chocolate shapes," says Nelly.

Nelly came up with a

great gift!

Gilroy tries to make a chocolate shape.

Gilroy makes a mess instead.

"Don't worry, Gilroy. I know you'll find

the right thing to make," says Nelly.

On the way home, Llama Llama and

Gilroy visit Euclid.

Euclid is making little buildings out of

wooden sticks.

Wow!

"These buildings are

so amazing!" says

Llama Llama.

But Gilroy can't build anything like that for his friends.

He is not great at math like Euclid is.

"You have to figure out your *own* thing," says Llama Llama.

"I know that you will come up with something great!" says Euclid.

The Valentine's Day party is finally here!

"What amazing and original valentines!"

says Zelda Zebra.

"I made heart-shaped cookies for

everyone," says Llama Llama.

"You just have to use your imagination

on the heart part!" he says.

Everyone laughs and eats a cookie.

There is one more gift to give out.

It is a Valentine's Day card.

But these aren't just *any* Valentine's Day cards.

There are poems inside!

Llama Llama reads his card out loud.

It says he is a great friend.

"I love my poem!" he says.

"Did you get a poem, Gilroy?" asks Luna.

Gilroy shrugs.

Wait!

Llama Llama understands.

"It was *you*! You wrote the poems!"

Llama Llama shouts.

"This is what you made for Valentine's

Day," he says.

Gilroy smiles proudly.

"You told me to do something that was creative and *me*! And I love writing!" he says to Zelda Zebra.

"And you are so good at it! I hope you do a lot more of it," says Zelda Zebra.

What a special Valentine's Day.

Llama Llama and his classmates show

one another how much they care—*and*

they discover their own special talents!

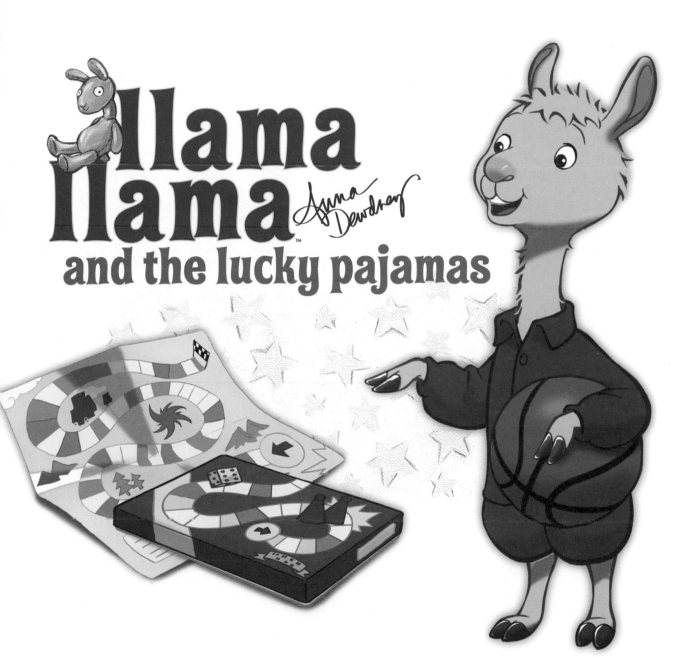

llama llama and the lucky pajamas

Anna Dewdney

Llama Llama plays in his bedroom one Saturday morning. He is wearing his red pajamas that Mama Llama just mended for him. He launches a basketball over his shoulder. It swishes through the hoop.

Llama rushes downstairs. "Mama!" he calls out. "I made the most *amazing* shot with my back turned!"

"Way to go!" says Mama. After they celebrate, Mama asks Llama to make toast for breakfast. Llama is worried that he'll burn the toast like he usually does.

They play Steps and Slides while they wait for the toast to be ready. Llama rolls the dice and cheers, "A six! I win!" He twirls around the kitchen. Suddenly, he stops. "The toast!" he cries.

But the slices pop up perfectly golden

brown. Llama grins. "Things are going

really well today."

This makes Mama think of something. She digs in the closet and pulls out a goofy hat. Llama laughs.

"This hat brings me luck," Mama tells him.

"What's 'luck'?" asks Llama.

Mama explains that having good luck is when positive things happen to you. She hopes her lucky hat will help her find a parking space at the supermarket.

Llama's eyes light up. "You must have made my pajamas lucky when you mended them, Mama! That's why I had good luck with the basketball, the toast, and the game."

Llama decides to wear his lucky pajamas all day long.

Later, Llama's friends come over to play.

Nelly Gnu grins when Llama answers the

door. "Cool outfit, Llama!"

Euclid points out that Llama is wearing

pajamas.

Llama says, "Not just any pajamas—my *lucky* pajamas!" To prove how lucky they are, he suggests a game of hide-and-seek. They play, and Llama finds his friends, *one-two-three.*

"Amazing!" says Euclid. "You found all of us in a superfast flash!"

Euclid wants another test of the lucky pajamas. "What can you try that you've never done before?" he asks Llama.

"I know," says Llama, leading them outside. As they jump rope, Llama exclaims, "We're all jumping exactly together!"

Mama calls from the open window, "I made snacks."

"My favorite apple-honey crisps?" asks Llama.

"Yes," Mama says with surprise.

"How did you know?"

Llama laughs. "My

lucky pajamas,

of course!"

As they munch in the kitchen, Llama's friends ask if they can borrow his pajamas. They want good luck, too!

Mama Llama interrupts. "I think it's better if everyone sticks with their own clothes."

Then Luna has a brilliant idea. She's going to make her own lucky pajamas! Mama Llama has extra cloth, and everyone helps.

But when Luna holds up her new lucky
pajamas, they're huge and uneven. Luna
cuts them up so everyone can wear a piece.

On Monday, Llama Llama wears his
pajamas underneath his clothes to school.

He finds his friends on the playground.
Red pajama pieces are tied to Nelly's
forehead, Luna's hair, and Euclid's wrist.

"Yay!" Llama cheers. "We all wore our
lucky pajamas!"

Gilroy Goat overhears them
talking about how lucky their
day will be. He challenges them.

"Prove it!" he says.

The friends try jump-roping together.

But unlike the day before, their timing is
totally off.

Gilroy shakes his head and laughs.

The day only gets worse from there. First,

Llama Llama messes up in art class.

At lunch, they frown at servings of soggy,

squishy food.

On the

playground,

none of them are

chosen to swing

first on the new swings.

"I guess they are not-so-lucky red

pajamas!" teases Gilroy.

Nelly thinks for a moment and says,

"Maybe they're only lucky at your house,

Llama."

Everyone rushes to Llama's house after school. Llama does everything he did on Saturday, but nothing turns out right.

The basketball bounces off the rim.

The toast burns to a crisp.

He loses at Steps and Slides.

Llama is close to tears. "Why aren't my

lucky pajamas working anymore?"

Mama gives him a hug. "Llama Llama,

you actually *are* very lucky," she reminds

him.

"But nothing went right today," moans Llama.

"That may be," says Mama, "but there's something better and bigger than luck."

"What's that?" asks Llama.

"Being *fortunate*," replies Mama. "I am fortunate to have a wonderful home, kind friends . . . *and* a loving son—you!"

Llama Llama smiles brightly. "I'm fortunate

to have a mama like you!" Then he adds, "And

great friends, Gram and Grandpa, Fuzzy—

and mended red pajamas."

This gives Llama a great idea. "Let's make an 'I'm Lucky and Fortunate List'!" Everyone takes turns calling out the things they are glad to have. Llama draws pictures.

⭐ **Books!**

⭐ **Holidays!**

⭐ **Warm wool hats!**

⭐ **Our families!**

⭐ **Hot cocoa with marshmallows!**

⭐ **Our school!**

⭐ **Yummy pancakes!**

Llama Llama smiles. He is very lucky

and fortunate to be making this special list

with his wonderful friends.

llama llama loves camping

"I'm excited to go camping tomorrow!"

Llama Llama tells his friends. He has never

camped overnight before. Neither has

Nelly Gnu, Luna, Gilroy, or Euclid.

"It will be super fun," Mama Llama says.

"And Grandma Llama and I will be with you

the whole time."

"Camping is going to be very different from being at home," says Llama.

Luna nods. "We'll be out in the open, under the trees and sky."

"And we won't have any kitchen or house things, like a refrigerator, an oven, or lights," says Gilroy.

Euclid looks worried. After all, he loves gadgets. "We can't use any machines while we camp?" he asks.

"That's right," says Mama Llama. "We are just going to bring the essentials. *Essentials* are the few things we really need. But don't worry, Euclid. It's only for one day and night!"

The next day is warm and sunny as the campers arrive at the campground.

"Welcome to our overnight adventure in the woods!" says Grandma Llama.

Llama Llama and his friends cheer loudly.

Everyone has one bag, except for Euclid.

He's carrying two!

"Don't worry," he explains. "I only

brought the essentials."

"That's a lot of essentials!" Nelly says

with a laugh.

"Okay, campers," says Mama Llama. "Let's go for a hike while it's still light outside!"

Euclid pulls a handheld gadget out of one of his bags. "I can plug our route into my directional device," he says.

"Remember, Euclid," Llama says kindly, "no gadgets allowed."

Euclid sighs. "Okay," he says, putting it away. "Not using gadgets isn't going to be easy!"

Mama Llama leads the campers along a trail in the woods.

"Wow," says Llama, looking around.

"These trees are so tall!"

"I wonder how tall they are," Euclid says.
"Can I measure them with my digital tape measure?"

Luna shakes her head. "No gadgets," she reminds him.

"Oh, yeah," Euclid says.

When the group gets farther into the

woods, Mama Llama asks the campers

to stop for a moment. "Let's listen to the

sounds of nature," she says. "What do you

hear?"

Llama pauses. "I hear a bird chirping," he says.

"I hear leaves rustling," says Luna.

"I hear a tree creaking," says Gilroy.

Nelly points to a bee. "I hear him buzzing," she says.

"I hear all that, too," says Euclid. "And I hear water flowing in the distance."

"The sounds in the woods are very different from the sounds at home," says Luna.

"Yeah," says Nelly. "Those are machine sounds. *Beep! Ring, ring! Wee-ooo, wee-ooo!*" She laughs at her imitation of a siren.

Euclid pulls a tape recorder and a camera from his bag. "I want to make a recording to remember the sounds," he explains.

Mama Llama smiles at Euclid. "For this trip, let's just listen hard to remember everything," she says.

"I forgot," says Euclid. "This no-gadgets thing is tougher than I thought."

After their hike, Llama and his friends

help Mama Llama and Gram set up camp.

Instead of a house, they have a tent.

Instead of a refrigerator, they have a cooler

with ice. And instead of an oven, they have

a roaring campfire!

"It takes some work to camp out," says

Mama Llama. "But it helps you appreciate

the nice things you have at home a little

more."

Later, the campers eat a delicious

dinner around the fire. "And now it's time

for dessert!" says Grandma Llama, handing

out sticks.

"Do we just eat these?" asks Gilroy.

"No," says Gram, laughing. "You eat

these marshmallows after we roast them

in the fire!"

As the sun sets, everyone roasts marshmallows over the fire. They taste delicious—even better than a dessert you make at home!

"It's getting pretty dark out," says Nelly.

"It is," says Euclid. "But it's pretty nice roasting marshmallows in nature," he adds. "With no gadgets!"

Finally, it's time for bed. Inside the tent, the campers get cozy in their sleeping bags. Once they're all tucked in, Mama Llama has an idea. "Let's listen closely to the sounds outside and pretend they're music," she says.

The campers close their eyes. They hear crickets chirping. They hear a bird calling. They hear the wind whooshing and an owl hooting.

"It sounds like they're all talking to each other," says Llama.

The music of the forest is very peaceful. As they listen to the nighttime sounds, the campers slowly drift off to sleep.

157

In the morning, sunlight streams into
the tent. The campers wake up feeling
refreshed. Mama Llama and Gram are
very proud of Llama and his friends for
spending the entire night in the woods.

But everyone is especially proud of Euclid. "Good job!" cheers Llama Llama. "You didn't use any gadgets on our campout!"

"Thank you," Euclid says. "It was a fun challenge. I like the woods!" The other campers agree.

"Can we go on another hike before we leave?" Nelly asks.

"We sure can," says Grandma Llama. "But first, breakfast!"

"We can use my electric waffle maker!" says Euclid. "Oh, wait," he adds. "That's kind of a gadget, isn't it?" He's made it this far without using machines. He isn't going to stop now!

llama llama happy birthday!

Anna Dewdney

Llama Llama wakes up with a smile on his face. He hops right out of bed. "Fuzzy!" he says to his stuffed llama. "It's my birthday! I can't wait to play with all my friends."

Downstairs, Mama Llama greets Llama
Llama with a big hug—and a delicious
pancake cake. "Happy birthday, Mama's
precious llama," she says.

Then Mama hands Llama Llama a birthday present. "This is for you!" she says. Llama tears it open.

"A toy airplane! Wow!" exclaims Llama Llama. "Thank you, Mama. My friends are going to be so excited to play with my new plane."

First, Llama Llama goes next door to Nelly Gnu's house. "I got this new plane for my birthday," he tells her. "Want to play?"

"I can't," says Nelly. "I have to help my mama with my little brother. Sorry, Llama Llama."

Llama Llama spots Luna Giraffe in her front yard. "Do *you* want to play with my new airplane?" Llama asks.

"I, um, can't," Luna says. "I have chores to do."

Llama goes to Euclid's house next. But he can't play, either.

"Sorry, Llama Llama," says Euclid. "I have to . . . count the blades of grass in the yard."

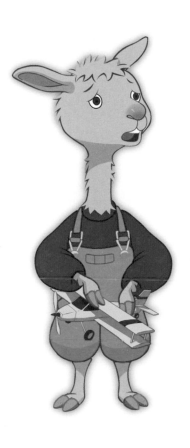

Llama Llama is disappointed that his friends are busy on his birthday. Luckily, Mama Llama can play! They toss Llama's airplane back and forth. Then—whoosh!— it zooms into Luna's backyard.

Llama knocks on Luna's front door. "Hi, Luna! My plane went in your backyard," Llama Llama explains. "Can I go get it?"

"No!" says Luna, pulling the front door closed. "I'll get it."

Luna finds Llama Llama's plane. She slides it back to him through a crack in the door.

"Sorry you can't play," says Llama Llama. "Maybe Nelly's free now," he says to himself.

As soon as Llama Llama
is out of sight, Luna races
to Nelly's house. Llama's
friends are all there. And
they're up to something
secret!

"Llama Llama
is coming!"
she tells them.
"Let's go!" They
hurry off as fast
as they can.

But all Llama Llama sees is his friends
running away! He doesn't understand.
"I thought they were all so busy," he
says sadly.

Back at home, Llama Llama tells his

Mama and Grandma Llama what happened.

"It looked like they were having fun," says

Llama. "I feel left out."

"I understand, honey," says Mama Llama.

"But things aren't always what they seem."

Llama Llama frowns. "It seemed like they were playing without me on my birthday," he says.

"Your friends would never leave you out on purpose," says Mama Llama.

"You're right," says Llama Llama. *But what were they doing?* he wonders.

Meanwhile, Llama Llama's friends are

back together in Nelly's yard. It turns

out they really *are* busy. But they aren't

playing without Llama Llama. They're

planning a surprise party for him!

"I would go play with Llama Llama, but I have to blow up the bouncy house," says Euclid.

"And I'm not done decorating," says Luna.

Gilroy Goat has an idea. They can play with their friend *and* plan his party. "I'll go play with Llama Llama first," he says.

When Gilroy finds Llama Llama,

Llama Llama is surprised to see him.

"What are you doing here?" asks Llama.

"I thought you were so busy, just like

everyone else."

"I *was* busy," says Gilroy, "but I can play

now. Let's go to the park!"

Together, Llama Llama and Gilroy make up a new game. "One, two, three . . . go!" says Llama Llama. Llama flies his plane while Gilroy kicks his ball. It's so much fun!

Suddenly, Luna appears. But Gilroy is gone! "Gilroy's mom needed him," says Luna. "I can play now!"

Llama and Luna play for a little while. Then Roland Rhino shows up. "I have to go home," says Luna. "See you soon!"

"I'm finally getting to play with my friends on my birthday," says Llama Llama. "Just not all at once, I guess!"

Soon, Nelly rolls up on her skateboard.

"Let's go to my house to play," she says.

"How about a fun ride home?" Nelly and

Roland push Llama Llama all the way to

Nelly's house.

"I'm not sure what this new game is,"

Llama Llama says with a giggle. "But I like

it already!"

When they get to Nelly's house, Llama

sees balloons and streamers and presents

everywhere. "Wow," says Llama Llama. "It

looks like you're getting ready for a super

fun party!"

Llama Llama's friends and family jump
out of their hiding spots. "Surprise!" they
all shout.

Llama can't believe it! "This is *my*
party?" he asks.

Nelly puts a party hat on Llama Llama's head.

"Now I know why everyone was so busy," Llama tells his friends. "You were planning a surprise party for me!"

"We would never leave you out," says Nelly. "Especially on your birthday!"

"I'm sorry I couldn't tell you," says Mama Llama. "But I didn't want to ruin the surprise."

Llama Llama gives her a big hug. "It's okay," he says. "I love surprises."

Llama Llama blows out the candle on

his birthday cake, and everyone cheers.

Happy birthday, Llama Llama!